D0842387

25748958

SACK LUNCH

Written by Bob and Nancy Reese
Illustrated by Bob Reese

CHILDRENS PRESS®

CHICAGO

Thanks to my wife, Nancy, for her ideas and help in writing "School Days." A special thanks also to Fran Dyra for her inspiration and editing.

WHITE MOUNTAIN LIBRARY
SWEETWATER COUNTY LIBRARY SYSTEM
ROCK SPRINGS, WYOMING

WM
J
Juc
Rees
8.95

Library of Congress Cataloging-in-Publication Data

Reese, Bob.
  Sack lunch / written by Bob and Nancy Reese,
illustrated by Bob Reese.
    p.   cm. — (School days)
  Summary: As a young girl makes her school lunch,
she learns which foods are better for her.
  ISBN 0-516-05582-8
  [1. Schools—Fiction. 2. Food habits—Fiction.
3. Stories in rhyme.] I. Title. II. Series.
PZ8.3.R255Sac   1992
[E]—dc20   92-12183
                                                     CIP
                                                      AC

Copyright © 1992 by Childrens Press®, Inc.
All rights reserved. Published simultaneously in Canada.
Printed in the United States of America.
1 2 3 4 5 6 7 8 9 10 R 01 00 99 98 97 96 95 94 93 92

WELCOME TO
MISS NATALIE'S
CLASS-ROOM 21

You can make

your lunch today.

Is
a
jelly
sandwich
OK?

Yes, but a turkey
sandwich is better.

TEA   COFFEE   SUGAR   FLOUR

A
turkey
sandwich.

Potato chips
or carrot sticks?

Potato chips are OK,
but carrot sticks are better.

WHITE MOUNTAIN LIBRARY
SWEETWATER COUNTY LIBRARY SYSTEM
ROCK SPRINGS, WYOMING

17

Punch is OK,
but milk is better.

Cake is OK,
but an apple is better.

SCHOOL
BUS
STOP

21

Do you want some cake today?

No, cake is OK, but
an apple is better.

WORD LIST

a	is	sandwich
an	jelly	some
apple	lunch	today
are	make	turkey
better	milk	want
but	no	yes
cake	OK	you
can	or	your
carrot sticks	potato chips	
do	punch	

About the Authors

Bob and **Nancy Reese** live in the mountains of Utah with two dogs and five cats. They have two daughters, Natalie who is a resource teacher in Utah and Brittany who is studying to be a dancer in New York City.

Bob worked for Walt Disney and Hanna Barbera studios and has a BA degree in art and business. Nancy is an interior decorator. Most of their ideas for books come from travels across the country.

SWEETWATER COUNTY LIBRARY SYSTEM
ROCK SPRINGS, WYOMING

39092 02947846 0

WHITE MOUNTAIN LIBRARY
SWEETWATER COUNTY LIBRARY SYSTEM
ROCK SPRINGS, WYOMING

3-95

BEGINNER

WHITE MOUNTAIN LIBRARY
2935 SWEETWATER DRIVE
ROCK SPRINGS, WY 82901
362-2665

WM J EASY REES
39092029478460
REESE, BOB.
SACK LUNCH

RD S